P9-BZX-721

GOONEY
the Fabulous

LOIS LOWRY

Illustrated by Middy Thomas

Houghton Mifflin Company Boston 2007

Walter Lorraine Books

For Schuyler and Gabrielle Small. —L.L.

For Rhys Avery Harrison, a fabulous little girl. —M.T.

Walter Lorraine *wn* Books

Text copyright © 2007 by Lois Lowry
Illustrations by Middy Thomas © 2007 by Houghton Mifflin Company

www.houghtonmifflinbooks.com

Library of Congress Cataloging-in-Publication Data
Lowry, Lois.
  Gooney the fabulous / Lois Lowry ; illustrated by Middy Thomas.
     p. cm.
  "Walter Lorraine books."
  Summary: Gooney Bird Greene takes charge of a class project as she and her fellow
students in Mrs. Pidgeon's second grade class learn about fables by each making up
their own based on an animal that begins with the same letter as their first name.
  ISBN-13: 978-0-618-76691-8
  ISBN-10: 0-618-76691-X
  [1. Authorship—Fiction. 2. Fables—Fiction. 3. Schools—Fiction. 4. Humorous stories.]
I. Thomas, Middy Chilman, 1931- ill. II. Title.
  PZ7.L9673Goo 2007
  [Fic]—dc22

                                                                    2006035594

Printed in the United States of America
MP 10 9 8 7 6 5 4 3 2 1

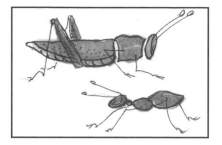

1.

"And so," Mrs. Pidgeon said, reading the final page of the book she was holding, "because the ant had worked very hard, he and his friends had food all winter. But the grasshopper had none, and found itself dying of hunger."

"Oh, no!" Keiko wailed. "I hate stories where people die!"

Malcolm, who had been rolling paper into balls while he listened to the story, tossed a little paper pellet at Keiko. "It's not people," he pointed out. "It's a dumb grasshopper! It's only a grasshopper! Just a grasshopper!"

"Nobody cares if a grasshopper dies!" Tyrone said.

"I do," Keiko murmured sadly. She folded her arms on her desk and then laid her head down on her arms.

"It's only a fable," Mrs. Pidgeon said. She held up the book. "*Aesop's Fables* is the title. Aesop was a man who lived a very long time ago. He was the creator of all of these fables. Tomorrow I'll read you another."

"Not about anybody dying!" Keiko implored, raising her head.

"No," Mrs. Pidgeon agreed. She leafed through the book. "I won't read 'The Wolf in Sheep's Clothing,' then, because I believe that one ends with the wolf eating the lamb—"

"Oh, noooo!" Keiko put her head back down and groaned.

"But I could read 'The Fox and the Grapes.' I think you'll enjoy that one, Keiko. You had some nice grapes in your lunch last week. I remember that you passed them around. That was very generous."

Keiko looked up and nodded. "Red seedless," she reminded everyone, "from my parents' grocery store. But Malcolm started a squishing contest, so I'm not bringing grapes ever again."

It was true. And unfortunately some of Mrs. Pidgeon's second-graders had joined in Malcolm's grape-squishing contest enthusiastically. Lester Furillo, the school custodian at the Watertower Elementary School, had had to come in during recess with his Shop-Vac to clean the floor of the multipurpose room where the children ate their lunch each day.

Mrs. Pidgeon placed the Aesop book upright, so the cover was visible, on top of the bookcase near the windows. "Time for social studies," she said. "But first, who would like to tell me what the moral is in 'The Ant and the Grasshopper'? Hands, please."

She looked around. "Barry Tuckerman?" As usual, Barry's hand was waving in the air.

"What's a moral?" Barry asked.

"My goodness," Mrs. Pidgeon said, "I should have explained that! Every fable has a moral. A moral is . . . " She hesitated.

Then she said, "Class, this is an opportunity to use our new dictionaries!"

She wrote the word on the board: MORAL.

The room was silent for a moment except for the sound of pages turning, as all the second-graders looked through the brand-new dictionaries that they had recently been given.

Gooney Bird Greene found it first and raised her hand. She was wearing fingerless gloves today, and a long flannel dress with a ruffle around the bottom; it looked suspiciously like a nightgown. Gooney Bird was known for her unusual outfits.

When Mrs. Pidgeon pointed to her, Gooney Bird stood and read aloud, "'A conclusion about how to behave, based on events in a story.'"

"Good dictionary work, Gooney Bird," said the teacher. "And so what was the moral of the fable about the ant and the grasshopper? What was the conclusion about how to behave?"

Gooney Bird rolled her eyes. "I could tell you," she said, "but I think it would be better if Malcolm did, because Malcolm is the one who *needs* advice on behavior!"

Mrs. Pidgeon chuckled. "Malcolm?" she said, pointing to him. He had the lid of his desk raised, and was shuffling the papers inside.

"What?" he asked, looking out from behind the raised lid.

"Could you tell us, please, what behavior we learned from the fable I just read?"

"Huh?"

Mrs. Pidgeon jiggled her knee. She always did that when she felt impatient. "Malcolm," she said, "I just read the class a

story, a fable, actually, about a grasshopper and an ant. Maybe you didn't listen well. The ant worked very hard collecting and storing food, while the grasshopper just played and chirped. Then when winter came, the ant and his fellow ants all had plenty to eat, but the grasshopper—"

"Starved!" Keiko wailed. *"And died!"*

Tricia reached over and patted Keiko's back, to comfort her.

"So, Malcolm," Mrs. Pidgeon went on, "what do we learn from the story?"

Malcolm thought. "Don't step on ants," he said at last. "If ants are there, don't step on them. Never step on ants."

Mrs. Pidgeon sighed. She was silent for a long time. Everyone had noticed that Malcolm had recently begun saying everything three times. He couldn't seem to help it. They were all trying to ignore it, but sometimes it was difficult. The second-graders watched Mrs. Pidgeon. Finally she said, "Let's get out our social studies books, class. Turn to the chapter called 'Cities and Towns,' please."

"Wait!" called Malcolm. "I know! Clean up your crumbs after lunch or your kitchen will be full of ants! Don't leave your crumbs around! Wipe up any crumbs!"

"That's page thirty-two, class," Mrs. Pidgeon said. She held up the social studies book, open to a picture of a city filled with skyscrapers.

"Felicia Ann?" she said. "Did I see your hand up?"

Felicia Ann, looking at the floor, nodded. She was the shyest person in Mrs. Pidgeon's second grade. She never looked up. She rarely spoke above a whisper.

"Did you want to say something?" the teacher asked her.

"Yeth, pleathe," whispered Felicia Ann. She had recently lost her two front teeth.

"Listen, class," Mrs. Pidgeon said, and held her finger in front of her mouth so that the children would be quiet.

"Work hard and don't play all the time," Felicia Ann said, blushing. "Plan ahead. Then you'll be ready for anything! A flood, or a blitherd—"

"What's a blitherd?" asked Beanie. "I never heard of a blitherd."

"She means blizzard," Gooney Bird explained.

"Yeth," Felicia Ann agreed. "Blitherd. And that'th the moral!" She looked up shyly and grinned.

"I liked the fable," she added, and looked at the floor again.

"Good," said Mrs. Pidgeon. "All right, class. Now we'll—"

"I don't get it!" Malcolm called out. "That story wasn't about floods or blizzards! It was insects! It was about insects! It was a story about insects! Ants! One time I was at my cousin's house and I sat on a whole hill of red ants, and—"

He was wiggling in his seat. Mrs. Pidgeon went to him and put her arm firmly across his shoulders. "Get a grip," she said. Sometimes she had to do that to calm Malcolm down. Sometimes Malcolm had to have a time-out. Malcolm had a hard time being calm at school, because at home his family had baby triplets and life was never calm. Their house, Malcolm said, was filled with the noise of babies crying, and their bathroom was filled with the smell of laundry, mostly in threes: three sets of baby clothes with spit-up on the front; and their kitchen was filled with groups of three bottles and three sippy cups and spilled milk and half-empty jars of strained peas, and sometimes Malcolm's mother announced, "I am going to scream three times!" and then she did, and after that she felt better for a while.

Now the class waited, as they were accustomed to doing, until Malcolm got a grip. Then they took out their social studies books and turned to page 32.

All but Gooney Bird Greene. Her social studies book was on her desk, but she hadn't opened it.

"Mrs. Pidgeon?" Gooney Bird raised her hand, and when the teacher nodded to her, she said, "I have a great idea!"

The second-graders, including Malcolm, all cheered. Whenever Gooney Bird had a great idea, something exciting was about to happen.

2.

At lunchtime, in the multipurpose room, all of Mrs. Pidgeon's second-graders sat together and traded lunch parts, as they always did.

"Anyone want some of my sushi?" asked Gooney Bird Greene. "This one is called *kappa maki*. It's mostly cucumber." She held up a small glistening cylinder.

"What's that green stuff?" Barry asked, making a face.

"Nori," Goony Bird told him.

"That's seaweed," Keiko explained.

"Yuck," Barry replied.

"You shouldn't have told him it was seaweed, Keiko," Gooney Bird said. "He might have thought it was spinach. Oh, well. I like it. I'll eat it myself." She popped the *kappa maki* into her mouth.

"Anyone want half a cream cheese and jelly on raisin bread?" Beanie asked. She held up a triangle of her sandwich.

"I'll take it, if the jelly isn't mooshing out," Chelsea said. "Let me see." She examined the sandwich half carefully.

8

"Okay. I'll give you five carrot slices and an oatmeal cookie for it."

All around the table the second-graders made their trades. "YESSS!" Malcolm said suddenly. He was looking down at his lunch. "YESSS! YESSS!"

"Malcolm has all dessert!" Beanie pointed out. "How did you do that, Malcolm?"

He grinned happily at his pile of three cookies and three plastic cups of chocolate pudding. "Traded away two halves of an egg salad sandwich and an apple," he explained, talking with his mouth full. "I traded—"

Gooney Bird interrupted him before he could describe it three times. "Where's your lunch, Nicholas?" Gooney Bird asked. Nicholas often brought KFC chicken pieces, and sometimes he let her trade for one.

"I gave it away," Nicholas said. He looked gloomy.

"Why?"

"I'm not hungry."

"Are you sick?" Gooney Bird asked sympathetically. "We could take you to the nurse's office."

"No, I'm okay," Nicholas said. But he put his head down in his arms, on the table.

Around them, the other classes were also eating and talking. It was December. Christmas, Hanukkah, and Kwanzaa decorations were on the walls. Mr. Leroy, the principal, had been wearing holiday neckties now for several days; today he was wearing one with small menorahs on it. Yesterday's had been reindeer. The kindergarten children had pasted photographs of

themselves onto circles of construction paper and made a long chain of the dangling pictures that hung across the tops of the multipurpose room windows. The kitchen workers were all wearing Santa hats. And the school dog, a Saint Bernard named Bruno who belonged to Lester Furillo, the custodian, didn't seem to mind wearing plastic antlers. The whole school had a feeling of excitement because the holidays were coming.

"We need to make a sign," Beanie said, chewing on a carrot stick, "announcing the you-know-what."

Nicholas looked up briefly, then put his head back down.

"Yes! Our you-know-what!" Ben agreed. With a swat of his hand he flattened his empty milk carton.

"Our *fabulous* you-know-what!" added Chelsea as she wadded up her napkin and threw it, unsuccessfully, toward the trash can.

The fabulous you-know-what was Gooney Bird's idea.

"We can write our own fables!" Gooney Bird had explained. "We already know how to write good stories—"

"Create interesting characters!" Ben announced.

"Describe them carefully so they seem real," Tricia added.

"Make them talk! That's called dialogue!" Barry called out.

"Put in a beginning, a middle, and an end," Tyrone said. Then he went into his rap routine. *"First you gotta start cuz you gotta have heart, and next you gotta middle cuz you feelin' like a fiddle, and when you gonna end everybody be yo' friend*—" He stood at his desk and moved his body.

"Go, Tyroooonnne!" Malcolm called. "Go! Go!"

Mrs. Pidgeon, smiling, went to Tyrone and placed her arm firmly over his shoulders. "You're good, Tyrone. You're really good! But save it till recess. Class, quiet down, please."

When the room was silent, Felicia Ann looked up and spoke in her shy, whispery voice. "And alwayth put in a thuddenly," she reminded the class.

"Suddenly," Mrs. Pidgeon announced, "I think we have an interesting project, compliments of Gooney Bird Greene!"

"Yay!" the second-graders shouted, and Gooney Bird, holding her long maybe-a-nightgown out to the sides, curtsied politely.

With the teacher's help, the class decided that the fable project would become, also, a holiday celebration for the school. They had time, they thought. There were still two weeks before vacation.

Each child would write a fable, an animal story, using an animal that matched his or her own initial.

"I could be a bull! B is for bull!" Ben called out, making horns out of his hands and leaning forward with a snort. He pawed the floor with one foot.

"I could be a tiger!" shouted Tyrone.

"Remember, though, each fable must have a moral!" Mrs. Pidgeon reminded them. "And a moral is what?"

They were all silent for a moment. Then Beanie raised her hand. "It's when you learn how to behave, from the story. I mean, from the fable."

"Good for you, Beanie. All right, class. Be thinking about

12

choosing your animal and creating your fable and its moral. And then, after we listen to your fables here in the class-room—"

She interrupted herself. "Nicholas? Is something wrong?"

Nicholas had his head down on his desk. He raised it slightly. "No," he said.

"Mrs. Pidgeon! Mrs. Pidgeon!" Chelsea was waving her hand in the air.

Mrs. Pidgeon nodded to her. "Yes, Chelsea?"

"Can we wear costumes? For our animals?"

The teacher hesitated. "We don't really have time for making elaborate costumes, I'm afraid. Remember what a mess it turned into at Thanksgiving, with all those Pilgrims and Native Americans?"

The class looked disappointed.

"I have an idea," Gooney Bird, who was still standing after her curtsey, said. "We don't need whole costumes. But just one little thing, to show the animal. Like if Ben's fable was about a bull, he could wear, oh, maybe a *tail* . . ."

All of the children shrieked with laughter. *"Ben's got a ta-il, Ben's got a ta-il,"* Malcolm called in a singsong voice. *"Ben's got a—"*

"I'm not being a bull," Ben said angrily. "I changed my mind. My fable's going to be about some other animal."

"Let's each keep our animal secret for now," Mrs. Pidgeon suggested. "Then, when our fables are ready, we can wear one thing—not a large thing—to indicate something about the animal. It doesn't have to be a tail," she added, looking at Ben.

13

"Will you do one, Mrs. Pidgeon?" Keiko asked.

"Certainly I will. I'm part of this class."

"You could be a pigeon!" Barry pointed out. "Can a bird be in a fable?"

"Of course," the teacher said. "Aesop wrote one about a crow.

"All of you start thinking. Right now we must turn to our social studies. But be thinking about your fables. And after they are all finished, on the last day of school before vacation, we can share them with the rest of the school by having a parade through the halls!"

"A parade of the animals!" Keiko said, and clapped her hands.

"A Fabulous Parade!" said Gooney Bird Greene.

3.

"Gooney Bird," suggested Mrs. Pidgeon, "I'm going to put you in charge of this, since it was your wonderful idea. Most of the children are ready. So would you come here to the front of the class and call on them?"

A week had passed. Now, with just one week left until vacation, the second-graders had been working with excitement on the project. Many of them had brought in their costume parts and were eager to display them and tell their fables.

Gooney Bird, who always looked as if she were wearing a costume even when she wasn't, came to the front of the classroom. Today she was wearing her hiking boots; two different-colored knee socks, one blue and one yellow, appeared at the top of the boots. Even though there was snow on the ground outdoors, Gooney Bird was wearing red plaid Bermuda shorts. She also wore a short-sleeved T-shirt in army camouflage colors, and dangling around her neck was a sparkly rhinestone necklace.

Mrs. Pidgeon went to sit in her desk chair. Then she said,

"Actually, Gooney Bird, maybe you'd like to go first, since it was your idea?"

Gooney Bird thought for a moment. Then she said, "No. I want to go last."

"All right then, you may go last. Time to choose who goes first!"

"Volunteers?" Gooney Bird asked, looking around the classroom. "Hands?"

Many hands shot into the air. Barry Tuckerman, as always, was half standing at his desk, waving his arm wildly. Felicia Ann, as always, was looking at the floor. But her hand was raised in a timid sort of way.

Gooney Bird looked at Nicholas. "Nicholas," she said, "you didn't raise your hand. But would you like to be first?"

Nicholas, who had been looking gloomy all week, shook his head.

"Is there anything we can do to make you feel more cheerful?" Gooney Bird asked in a kindly voice.

"No," Nicholas muttered.

"Well, then." Gooney Bird looked around the room at all the waving hands. Finally she looked at the teacher's desk. "Mrs. Pidgeon," she asked, "is your fable ready?"

"Yes," said Mrs. Pidgeon. "I have it right here."

"And your costume?" asked Gooney Bird.

Mrs. Pidgeon nodded.

"I'd like you to go first, then. You're a member of this class, after all."

Mrs. Pidgeon smiled. "All right," she said. She stood up. She was wearing black slacks and a black turtleneck shirt. She reached into the bag that she had stored under her desk and brought out a white vest and put it on.

"How shall we do this, Gooney Bird?" she asked. "Would it be fun to have the class guess what animal each of us is?"

"*No,*" Nicholas said loudly.

It was very startling. Nicholas ordinarily was a cheerful, outgoing boy. But all week he had been acting strangely.

Gooney Bird decided to ignore him. "Yes," she said, "let's guess. Class, take a look at Mrs. Pidgeon and guess what animal she is! Remember, it must begin with a P!"

"But P is for her *last* name," Tricia pointed out.

Mrs. Pidgeon laughed. "That's true," she said. But my first name is Patsy! I'm a two-P person! Now see if you can guess my animal."

The class all looked carefully. Mrs. Pidgeon was entirely black except for her white middle.

"*Penguin!*" the children all shouted.

"I saw *March of the Penguins*!" Beanie called out.

"Me too!" Malcolm said. "I did too! I saw it too! I saw *March of the Penguins*!"

"So did I!" called Ben. "My dad took me!"

"I saw it!" Chelsea said loudly.

"I thaw it too," Felicia Ann whispered, "but it wath tho thad!"

"Shhhhh," Gooney Bird said, and she held her finger in front of her mouth. "I'm sure Mrs. Pidgeon's fable won't be sad. Will it, Mrs. Pidgeon?" Gooney Bird stepped aside so that the

18

teacher could stand at the front of the class to read her fable.

Mrs. Pidgeon was laughing. "No," she said, "it isn't sad at all. But it also isn't about a penguin!"

"It isn't?" asked Gooney Bird, looking puzzled.

"No. I'm going to write the name of my animal on the board. I'm afraid guessing is not going to be a good idea. It might take forever. Instead, each of us can write our animal in a list. I'll start right here." Mrs. Pidgeon picked up the chalk and held it to the board. "Then, after we're all done," she said, "we can have a lesson in alphabetizing. Remember my beginning letter, P?"

She wrote an uppercase P on the board.

Then she added an A, an N, a D, and another A.

"Panda!" the class called out. They looked at their teacher again. Her arms and legs were black, and her middle was white. A perfect panda.

"Now," Mrs. Pidgeon said, "I'll read my fable."

Once there was a small panda who lived in a bamboo grove in China. He was a happy panda who spent his days playing in the tall stalks of bamboo and nibbling at the leaves.

One day a majestic deer wandered into the bamboo grove.

"Hello," said the deer to the panda. "You look as if you are enjoying your nibbling."

"Yes," the panda replied. "I am."

"I myself prefer to eat the tips of rhododendrons,"

the deer said. "They are quite yummy, and I think they have a lot of vitamins."

"Bamboo is yummy, too," said the panda, "but I'd be happy to give a rhododendron a try, on your recommendation."

So the majestic deer led the small panda out of the bamboo grove and through a meadow, then to a rhododendron bush at the edge of the woods.

"Here," said the deer. "Help yourself."

The panda nibbled curiously. The taste was not bad. It was very different from bamboo leaves. He ate several twigs and a few blossoms.

But suddenly his stomach began to hurt. He felt sick.

"I think I want to go home now," he called out to the deer. But the deer had gone away. The panda was alone, and lost.

With a badly aching stomach, and crying a bit because he was frightened, the panda found his way with much difficulty back to the bamboo grove.

He made himself comfy there and decided never to leave the bamboo grove again.

"That's the end," Mrs. Pidgeon said. She folded her paper, placed it on her desk, and smiled at the class.

"It wath a good fable," Felicia Ann said.

"Not too scary," Keiko added. "Just a little scary, at the *suddenly* part, when his stomach hurt. But *suddenlys* are almost always a little scary."

"Nicholas?" Mrs. Pidgeon said. "Did you enjoy it?"

Nicholas lifted his head briefly. "It was okay," he muttered.

"Thank you, Mrs. Pidgeon. You may take your seat," Gooney Bird said. She was very good at being in charge.

"Now, class," she went on, "who can tell the moral of Mrs. Pidgeon's panda fable?"

All of the children were silent, thinking of the story of the panda. "Put on your thinking caps," Gooney Bird reminded them.

Malcolm's hand shot up. "I know!" he called out. "I know what it is! Oh, I know—"

"Malcolm?" Gooney Bird pointed to him. "Would you tell us the moral? And by the way, you only need to say it one time."

Malcolm stood up at his desk. "Don't ever, ever go off with some stranger who offers you candy!" he announced loudly. "Remember not to go—"

"*Thtranger danger,*" Felicia Ann murmured, interrupting Malcolm.

"Oh dear," Keiko said. "That's scary."

Mrs. Pidgeon stood up. "That's a good reminder, Malcolm. But it's not exactly the moral I was thinking of. I'm going to tell you my fable's moral so that you'll all get the hang of it.

"The moral of the panda fable is this: *Sometimes what you already have is the best thing.*"

The children were silent for a moment, thinking it over.

"I get it!" Ben said. "Like when I got new hockey skates, but my old ones were really more comfortable!"

"And when my dad got his new car?" Chelsea added. "He said

he really liked the old one better even though it had a hundred million miles on it!"

"And my mom and dad!" Malcolm called. "They already had *me!* I was already their kid! They'd had me for seven years! But then they got—"

Mrs. Pidgeon went to Malcolm and put her hand on his shoulder. At the same time she reached with her other hand to Nicholas, and rubbed his back in a comforting way. Nicholas didn't look up.

"Gooney Bird," Mrs. Pidgeon said, "we have a lot of fables to get through. How about calling on the next person?"

Gooney Bird nodded, and looked around the room.

"Keiko?" she said. "You next."

4.

Keiko stood. She reached under her desk, picked up a pink canvas backpack, and put her arms through the straps. But she did it backwards, so that the pack was suspended against her chest. Then she walked to the front of the classroom.

The class began to laugh. "I know!" "I get it!" they called out.

Keiko went to the board, and under PANDA, in her best uppercase printing, she wrote:

KANGAROO

Then she turned to the class, unfolded her paper, and announced, "My fable is called—"

She interrupted herself and looked over at Mrs. Pidgeon and at Gooney Bird, who was standing beside the teacher's desk. "Are we supposed to have a title?" she asked.

"Oh, yes," Gooney Bird said. "All stories have titles."

"But Mrs. Pidgeon's fable didn't have a title!" Chelsea called.

"Uh-oh," said Mrs. Pidgeon. "I forgot. And Gooney Bird is right; all stories should have titles. See? Not even teachers are perfect!"

The second-graders, all but Nicholas, laughed.

"Of course, they are *almost* perfect," Mrs. Pidgeon added, and the class, all but Nicholas, laughed again.

"The title of my fable," Mrs. Pidgeon said, "was, ah, 'The Panda in the Bamboo Grove.' But now it's Keiko's turn. Go on, Keiko."

Keiko nodded and began again. "The title of my fable is 'The Kangaroo Who Came Home.'"

Once a very small kangaroo hopped out of his mother's pouch and went off to play.

He played with a koala and a dingo and a wallaby. They played tag and hide-and-seek.

Then it got late. It was time for supper. The animal friends said goodbye to each other and started for their homes.

But the baby kangaroo could not find his home! He had not been watching. His mother had hopped away across the dry land through the scratchy grass. He could not see her anymore. He did not know where she had gone.

He began to cry.

The koala said, "Come with me to my eucalyptus tree. You can share my dinner and sleep in my tree tonight."

So the kangaroo went with the koala. But he couldn't climb like the koala, and the tree was full of sharp twigs. It was very uncomfortable, and he did not like the taste of eucalyptus at *all*.

So he cried again.

The dingo said, "Come with me. I live in a small cave in those rocks over there. You can share my dinner and sleep in my cave."

The kangaroo tried that. But the dingo was eating rabbit for dinner, and the kangaroo was a vegetarian. He couldn't eat rabbit. And the cave was cold, not comfy and warm like his mother's pouch.

So he cried again.

The wallaby said, "Well, I can take you to where I live. As you know, I am a kind of kangaroo myself, so I eat leaves and roots the way you do. But I'm afraid there is no room in my mother's pouch for an extra. You will have to sleep on the ground, and it will not be cozy."

The little kangaroo cried and cried.

Suddenly he heard a thumping sound. He looked up. It was his own mother, leaping with her strong legs and big feet toward him. She had been looking everywhere.

He hopped to her and right into her pouch, which was warm and snug. There was milk waiting for him.

His mother scolded him gently and he promised never to wander away again, at least not until he was big.

Then he went happily to sleep.

"That's the end," Keiko said. "Did you like it?"

The second-graders clapped. They had liked her fable very much.

"It was a happy *suddenly,* when he heard his mom coming," Beanie pointed out, "not a scary one."

"Yes," Keiko said. "I wouldn't put in anything scary."

"Happy *suddenlys* are just fine," Gooney Bird told the students. "I think I may put one into *my* fable, actually. Thank you for that idea, Keiko."

She looked around. "Now," she said, "thinking caps! Who would like to tell us what the moral is? What kind of behavior are we supposed to learn from Keiko's fable?"

"Tricia?" Gooney Bird pointed to Tricia.

"Be a vegetarian!" Tricia said. "That's the moral!"

"My Aunt Carol is a vegetarian!" Barry called out. "My dad says she's a nutcase!"

"My mom's cousin Phyllis is a vegetarian!" shouted Chelsea. "And my mom says yeah, eat your dumb pumpkin casserole and more turkey for *us* at Thanksgiving!"

Mrs. Pidgeon stood up. "Class," she said, "many people are vegetarians. Nothing wrong with that. But I don't think that was the moral of the fable, was it, Keiko?"

Keiko shook her head. "No. And anyway, I like hot dogs."

"I have a feeling," Mrs. Pidgeon said, "that the moral of Keiko's fable is the same thing that we all remember from a certain movie. A movie that had a scarecrow and a tin man in it."

"The Withard of Oth," whispered Felicia Ann.

27

"I know!" Malcolm shrieked. "I know! Call on me! I know!"

"I'm going to call first on Nicholas, I think," Mrs. Pidgeon said.

Nicholas looked up. He frowned. But he gave the answer. *"There's no place like home,"* he said.

"Correct! And you know what?" Gooney Bird said. "In the movie, Dorothy says it three times! So we should have let Malcolm give the answer!"

"Go, Malcolm!" shouted Tyrone.

"There's no place like home! There's no place like home! There's no place like home!" Malcolm called out, with a big smile.

Then his smile changed to a scowl, and he added, "Unless the home has triplets."

5.

Beanie went to the front of the classroom to present her fable next. First she reached into her backpack and took out a small stuffed bear.

"This isn't really a costume, I guess," she said, "because I'm not *wearing* it. But my fable is about a bear, so I brought my old bear from home. I got him when I was born. His name is Teddy."

"That's a baby thing, to have a teddy bear when you're in second grade!" Barry said.

The class fell silent. Beanie looked embarrassed.

"Children?" Mrs. Pidgeon said, and she stood up. "When I was a very little girl, I had a stuffed lamb. I used to sleep with him. His name was Fleecy. And you know what?"

"What?" the class asked.

"I still have him. I don't sleep with him anymore. But Fleecy sits on a shelf in my bedroom, and I still love him just as much as I did all those years ago."

"I have a bear," Tricia said. "I call mine Bear-Bear."

"Tho do I," Felicia Ann whispered. "I thleep with my bear."

"I have a doll," Keiko said. "Not a bear. A soft doll with a painted face, and she is so old that her face is almost worn away, but I still love her just as much."

"I have a bunny," Ben said. "When I was born everybody gave me bunnies because of the story of Benjamin Bunny. My mom said I got eight bunnies when I was born. I only have one left, but I sleep with him every night, and when we went to visit my cousins and I forgot Bunny, I couldn't sleep."

Tyrone stood up. "Mine's a clown," he said. "My Nana made it. *Got me a clown and he never makes a frown, makes me laugh as much as a giraffe—*"

The class began to rap with Tyrone. *"Got me a clown—"*

"Enough," Mrs. Pidgeon said, laughing. "You'll get your turn, Tyrone, when you present your fable. But for now we want to hear Beanie's. And also, Barry?"

"What?"

"It isn't a baby thing at all, to have a bear. Or a lamb, or a doll, or a clown. I'd like you to apologize to Beanie."

"Sorry, Beanie," Barry said.

"That's okay." Still holding Teddy, Beanie turned and wrote BEAR on the list, just below KANGAROO. Then she unfolded her paper and read the title of her fable.

The Very Small Bear

Barry interrupted her. "Actually," Barry admitted, "I have a

stuffed walrus, and his tusks are all gross because I suck on them."

Mrs. Pidgeon put her finger to her mouth. "Shhhh," she said to Barry. "Let's be good listeners."

Once there was a mother bear with twin cubs. One was a big strong bear cub, and very brave. But the other was quite small and weak, and frightened of things.

When they went to the river so their mom could teach them to get fish, the big cub jumped right in and splashed around. He grabbed a salmon with his claws. But the little cub was afraid of the water, and he cried. "It's cold!" he said. "And I can't swim!"

The big cub made fun of the little one. "Sissy!" the bigger cub said, and grabbed another fish for himself.

When their mom took them to the orchard where sometimes she stole apples from the farmer's trees, the big cub jumped right up into a tree and grabbed apples and ate them with a gulp.

But the little cub only peeked out from his hiding place behind the corner of the barn. "What if the farmer sees us?" he said. "What if the farmer has a gun and *shoots* us?" It made him shake with fear just to think about it.

"Scaredy-cat!" said the big cub to his brother, and he stuffed another apple into his own mouth.

The mother bear took them to a dead tree she knew

of where she could get honey from a hive inside the trunk.

"Yay!" said the big cub. "Honey!" He climbed up the trunk of the tree, reached inside, and brought out his paw coated with sticky, delicious honey. The bees buzzed around angrily but he didn't care.

The little bear hid in the bushes and watched. He was very scared of bees. "What if they sting my nose?" he said.

So the big cub got bigger and bigger and healthier and healthier, but the little cub was always skinny and scared.

Beanie looked up. "That's the end," she said. "But it doesn't have a *suddenly*. And I don't think it has a moral, either."

Gooney Bird took the paper from Beanie and looked at it carefully. "You know what?" she said. "I don't think that was the end."

"It isn't?" Beanie said.

"You just stopped too soon," Gooney Bird pointed out.

"What if, after this last sentence—'the little cub was always skinny and scared'—you then added a *suddenly*?"

"But what could it say after that?" Beanie asked.

"Class?" Gooney Bird turned to the second-graders, who were all listening and thinking. "Ideas?"

Malcolm shouted, "Suddenly the big cub was killed by a lion and the little one got to eat all his food! This big lion comes and kills him, see! How about if a lion—"

"Oh, *no!*" wailed Keiko.

"Other ideas?" Gooney Bird asked.

"I have one," said Felicia Ann timidly.

"Remember, it should start with a *suddenly,*" Gooney Bird reminded her.

Felicia Ann nodded. "Thuddenly," she said, "the big cub got thtuck in a bear trap! He wath too fat to get out!"

"And then what?"

"Well, hith little brother came along and wath able to reach in and help him, becuth he wath thkinny! He unlocked the trap and let hith brother out!"

"YES!" called Tyrone. *"Caught in a trap cuz you acted like a sap, and along come your bro and help to let you go—"*

"Tyrone," said Mrs. Pidgeon, with a meaningful look.

"Sorry," Tyrone said.

"What do you think of Felicia Ann's suggestion?" Gooney Bird asked Beanie.

Beanie nodded happily. "I like it! And it has a moral!" she said.

"What's the moral?"

"Be nice to your brother!" Malcolm called out. "Always share with your brother! Your brother is—"

Mrs. Pidgeon put her hand firmly on Malcolm's shoulder. "Let Beanie answer," she said.

"Well," Beanie said slowly. *"Everybody has things they can do. You don't have to be big or brave. The important thing is to be helpful."*

"Sounds good to me!" Gooney Bird said. "Class? What do you think?"

"Sounds good!" the class said.

"The bear didn't die in the trap, did he?" Keiko asked fearfully.

"No," Beanie said. "He came out of the trap and went and got some fish and other stuff for his brother, to say thank you.

"The end," Beanie added.

6.

Felicia Ann went next.

"My fable ith very, very short," she said apologetically when she went to the front of the class.

"That's all right," Gooney Bird told her.

"You'll thee why," Felicia Ann said.

She was wearing a bright pink dress and matching pink tights. She went to the board. Carefully she printed, under BEAR, the word FLAMINGO.

Then Felicia Ann turned to the class and unfolded her paper. They could all see the very short sentences printed neatly on it.

"The title ith 'The Fable of the Flamingo,'" Felicia Ann read aloud.

Oneth there wath a flamingo. It didn't mind being bright pink.

But itth legs were pink, too. And that made it embarrathed. The flamingo thought that itth legth should be brown, like other birds' legth.

Tho it tried to hide them. It pulled one leg up to itth tummy in a folded way tho that no one would thee it.

But thuddenly, when it pulled the other leg up, it fell over.

Tho it only hid one leg at a time.

And it had a very hard time walking.

The end.

Everyone noticed that Felicia Ann was wobbling a bit. She had read her fable standing on one leg, with the other leg tucked up as high as possible.

After she read, "The end," she sighed with relief and put her leg down.

"I almotht tipped over," she said, "tho it had to be short."

"It was a good fable, though," Gooney Bird told her. "Class? Didn't you think so?"

The other second-graders, all but Nicholas, who was scribbling aimlessly on a piece of paper, nodded.

"And the moral?" Gooney Bird asked. "Do you want the class to guess, or would you like to tell us?"

"I'll tell the moral," Felicia Ann said shyly. "It'th thith: *You should be very proud of what color you are.*"

The class cheered and clapped.

"Even your legth," Felicia Ann added. She grinned. Then she went back to her desk.

Mrs. Pidgeon stood up. "Class," she said, "we have time for just one more fable before lunch, and then we'll do some more tomorrow.

"Nicholas?" she asked. "Would you like to be the final fable today?"

But Nicholas, looking miserable, shook his head no.

"Well," Mrs. Pidgeon said, "I can see that three of you—Chelsea, Malcolm, and Tyrone—are eager to have a turn. I wish you'd raise your hands with that much enthusiasm during math!

"Let's see. What do you think, Gooney Bird?"

"Well," Gooney Bird said, looking at the list on the board, "we've had three girls already today. So we should give a boy a turn."

Chelsea groaned and stopped waving her hand.

"And," Gooney Bird went on, "we've all been sitting and we probably could use the exercise. So let's let Tyrone do his. And let's all stand up for it.

"You too, Nicholas," Gooney Bird added, after the class had stood up but Nicholas was still slumped at his desk. Grudgingly, Nicholas stood.

With a grin Tyrone made his way to the front of the room. He carried no paper, but he had a shiny pie tin in his hand, and when he reached the front of the room, he hung the pie tin, which had a string attached to it in two places, around his neck.

"*My fable is*—" he began, his sneakers already tapping on the floor.

"Write your animal on the board!" Chelsea called. But Tyrone only grinned and moved his feet.

"Go ahead and yell it but I dunno how to spell it," he chanted, *"can't write it on the list cuz my spelling might be dissed, so I tell the story 'bout it and if you wanna you can shout it . . ."*

The whole class began to tap their feet and hum along with Tyrone. Even Nicholas looked up with interest.

The Tale of Tyrannosaurus Rex

You got it, it be TEEEE REX, TEEEE REX—okay for you to shout it cuz there ain't no way about it—this creature, he come along and he be so strong, sooo strong . . .

Tyrone twirled around and came to a stop, his pie tin dangling and bouncing on his chest.

. . . he got armor plates so no enemy can bite him, and he never gets in fights cuz everybody scared to fight him, and he taller than the trees and he never gets no fleas, and he don't say thank you and he don't say please, cuz he rule the earth since his mama give him birth . . .

"Lemme hear it!" Tyrone said, and the class, accustomed by now to his style, repeated the words. "Since his mama give

him birth, since his mama give him birth . . . "

There was a brief knock at the classroom door. It opened, and Mr. Leroy, the principal, appeared. He was wearing a tie that had candy canes on it, and some holly berries. "I heard some strange sounds from this classroom," he said, smiling, "and I suspected that the famous Tyrone was performing. May I sit in?"

He tiptoed over and sat down at Tyrone's empty desk. Mr. Leroy was a tall man, and sitting at a child's desk made his legs fold in an odd way, with his knees sticking up, but he never seemed to mind.

"It's a fable," Tricia whispered to him from the next desk. "Tyrone's doing a fable."

Tyrone continued.

Mr. Leroy don't be bitter, gonna hear about this critter, Teeee rex, Teeee rex . . .

"Teeee rex, Teeee rex," the class chanted. Mrs. Pidgeon and Mr. Leroy joined in.

He be one huge dude, every minute needin' food, and he's chompin' up the scene, eatin' everything that's green . . .

Tyrone danced across the open space at the front of the room, grabbing at imaginary things with his teeth, imitating a large animal grazing. "Lemme *hear* it!" he called, and the class, and Mrs. Pidgeon, and Mr. Leroy all chanted with him:

"Everything that's green, everything that's green!"

Then Tyrone stopped dancing, stood still, and lowered his voice to finish his fable.

Big T rex, he rule the earth and he rule the moon, but he be in trouble really soon, cuz one fine day as quick as a wink, he go to wake up and he now extinct.
EXXXXXTINCT!

Tyrone bowed while the class clapped and cheered, as they always did for Tyrone's performances. Mrs. Pidgeon, laughing, said, "Great as always, Tyrone. But haven't you forgotten something? What does a fable always have?"

"Gettin' to that," Tyrone explained. He turned to the class. "Wanna hear a moral?"

They nodded.

"I can't *hear* you!" Tyrone called. "Wanna hear a moral?"

"Wanna hear a moral!" the class chanted.

"Louder!"

"WANNA HEAR A MORAL!"

Tyrone resumed his position, tapped his feet, and finished his rap.

Big be nice, and big be cool, but big don't mean that you gonna rule, cuz here's the moral of ole T rex: *BIG MEAN NUTHIN' IF YOU DON'T DO SCHOOL!*

"School! School!" the class repeated, chanting and clapping.

"Well," said Mr. Leroy as he unfolded his long legs and stood up, "thank you, Tyrone. That made my day.

"Made my day," the principal chanted, dancing toward the door. "Made my day. *Big mean nuthin' if you don't do school.*" He disappeared, still chanting, into the hall.

Mrs. Pidgeon went to the board and wrote TYRANNO-SAURUS REX below FLAMINGO. "Now: lunchtime, class," she said with a smile.

7.

"Mrs. Pidgeon?" Tricia asked the teacher at lunch. Sometimes the teachers all sat together at a separate table, or even ate their lunch in the teachers' room. But today Mrs. Pidgeon was eating with the children. She had even made a trade, and given Gooney Bird a nice red apple in exchange for the five olives-stuffed-with-anchovy that Gooney Bird had brought as an hors d'oeuvre.

"I think lunch ought to have courses," Gooney Bird always said. "I like to have an appetizer—sometimes I call it the hors d'oeuvre—and a salad, and an entrée, and a dessert course. I'd do a soup course, too, but every time I've tried it, my soup has spilled before lunchtime. And I do hate it when my dessert gets wet."

Today Gooney Bird, to everyone's amazement, had taken something made of embroidered cloth out of her lunchbox. She unfolded it carefully and tied it around her neck.

"That's a bib!" Malcolm bellowed. "That's what babies wear! Babies wear bibs!"

"I know that," Gooney Bird replied calmly. "Actually, I bought this one in the baby section of the Goodwill store."

"But why would you wear a baby thing?" Beanie asked.

"It's sensible," Gooney Bird replied. "Babies wear bibs to keep their clothes clean. That's a sensible thing to do. I am a sensible person. So I have decided to wear a bib." She smoothed the bib over her chest. It had an embroidered duck on it.

"But aren't you embarrathed?" Felicia Ann whispered.

"I am never ever embarrassed," Gooney Bird replied.

Everyone was silent for a moment. Then Malcolm said, "We have a whole lot of bibs at home. A million bibs. We have—"

Mrs. Pidgeon interrupted him in a kindly way. "Time to eat, Malcolm," she said gently. Then she turned to Tricia. "Did you want to ask me something? I think we all got distracted by Gooney Bird's bib."

Tricia nodded. "Me and Ben—" she began. Then she stopped. Mrs. Pidgeon had held up a finger—she called it her grammar finger—as a reminder.

"Ben and I," Tricia corrected.

"Good. That is much better grammar," Mrs. Pidgeon explained.

"How come Tyrone can use bad grammar when he raps?" Malcolm asked. "And you never once hold up your grammar finger?"

"Ahhh," Mrs. Pidgeon said with a chuckle. "Good question, Malcolm. Rap is a special art form. And it uses a different grammar. So Tyrone can say, in a rap—well, give us an example, Tyrone, would you?"

Tyrone looked down at his lunch, a pear and a sandwich on a paper napkin in front of him. He thought for a moment, then chanted, *"Ain't no pear as big as my hair, cuz pears be small and my hair be tall . . ."*

Mrs. Pidgeon laughed. "All right," she said. "Now, Tyrone, tell us that in proper grammar."

Tyrone grinned. Then he said, "There isn't any pear as big as my hair, because pears are small, but I always comb my hair up to make it look pretty large."

"See the difference?" Mrs. Pidgeon asked, and the children nodded.

"So: what were you going to ask me, Tricia? About you and Ben?"

"Is it okay if Ben and I do our fable together?"

"Certainly."

"Because we were talking about our initials, and Ben was going to do BEAR, but Beanie already did. But we thought of a fable you already read to us, by Aesop—"

"Which one?" Mrs. Pidgeon asked.

" 'The Tortoise and the Hare,' " Tricia said.

All of the children nodded. "I remember that one!" Keiko said. "I liked that one."

"But there's no B animal in it!" Chelsea pointed out. "Tortoise. Hare. T and H."

Ben explained. "We're going to make it 'The Tortoise and

47

the Bunny.' T and B for Tricia and Ben."

"Bunny!" shrieked Chelsea. "Ben's going to be a *bunny!*"

"*Bunny*'s a baby word!" Malcolm said, sputtering with laughter. "Babies say 'bunny'! Bunny is—"

Mrs. Pidgeon put her calm-down hand on his shoulder. "But a minute ago," she said, "we were talking about bibs. Bibs can be called baby things. But look at Gooney Bird."

Everyone looked. Gooney Bird was still wearing her bib with the embroidered duck on it. "I have another bib at home," Gooney Bird said, "and I'll wear it tomorrow. It features a bunny."

"Good," Mrs. Pidgeon said. "And tomorrow Tricia and Ben can do their fable, 'The Tortoise and the Bunny.'"

"I am never ever embarrassed," Ben said proudly.

Walking back to the classroom after lunch, Nicholas trudged slowly, dragging his feet. The other children hurried ahead, all but Gooney Bird. She walked beside Nicholas. Mrs. Pidgeon, walking slowly too, took his hand.

"Nicholas," Mrs. Pidgeon said softly, "do you want to tell Gooney Bird and me what is wrong?"

Nicholas shook his head. But now they could see that there were tears on his cheeks.

Mrs. Pidgeon called to the rest of the children. "Go on into the classroom," she said, "and start studying your spelling words! I'll be there in a minute."

She knelt beside Nicholas. "You know," Mrs. Pidgeon said, "every single person has something that they feel upset about. It's one of the reasons that we read fables. They teach us about things."

Nicholas sniffled. He looked at the floor.

"For example, I know there are some children in my second grade who think they don't like school, and it isn't important.

"But Tyrone's fable about the T. rex had a moral, remember?"

Nicholas didn't look up. But he was listening. He shook his head.

"Gooney Bird? Do it with me?" Mrs. Pidgeon asked. Then she and Gooney Bird chanted together, *Big mean nuthin' if you don't do school!*

They could see Nicholas smile just a tiny bit.

"And," Mrs. Pidgeon went on, "let's see. Beanie's fable about the bear taught us that being the smallest doesn't make you less of a hero. Remember how the little cub saved his brother?"

Nicholas nodded.

"And Felicia Ann's taught us how to be proud of your color, didn't it?"

Nicholas nodded again. "Even your legth," he said, imitating Felicia Ann.

Mrs. Pidgeon chuckled. "Even your legth," she agreed.

Gooney Bird said, "And Malcolm. He's upset about those triplets. Maybe we could figure out a fable that would help Malcolm with that. Do you have your fable done yet, Nicholas?"

"No."

"Neither do I," said Gooney Bird. "I'm going last. But we could do one together, Nicholas! Would you like that?"

But surprisingly, Nicholas began to cry loudly. "I can't!" he sobbed.

"Why not?" asked Gooney Bird.

"Why not, sweetie?" asked Mrs. Pidgeon, patting his back.

Choking back the sobs, Nicholas told them the reason. "I don't have an animal!" he wailed.

"My goodness," Mrs. Pidgeon said. "That shouldn't be a problem!"

"It has to be an N!" Nicholas wept. "I thought and thought every day, and at night! I tried and tried, but there isn't one! I'm the only one who doesn't have an animal!"

"But what about a—" Then Mrs. Pidgeon hesitated for a long time, thinking, with a puzzled look on her face. "Oh, dear," she said at last. "It *is* a problem. Gooney Bird, what do you think? Can you come up with one?"

Gooney Bird, who felt that taking deep breaths was always helpful in problem-solving, took several deep breaths. She closed her eyes tightly, something she often did while thinking deeply.

Then she opened her eyes and grinned. "YES!" she said. "Got it!"

"What's the answer?" Mrs. Pidgeon asked.

Gooney Bird took Nicholas's hand. She tapped her foot the way Tyrone always did. "*You and me, me and you,*" she chanted. "*Gonna be a secret between us two, cuz the teacher dunno and the class dunno, but me and you, we be stars of the show!"*

Gooney Bird grinned. "You'll see, Mrs. Pidgeon," she said. "It'll be the best *suddenly* ever!"

8.

The words BUNNY and TORTOISE had now been added to the list on the board. Ben and Tricia had told the well-known story of the race between the two, the race won by the slow, plodding tortoise (Tricia, the tortoise, had worn old leather gloves, wrinkled and brown, on both hands and both feet) because the foolish hare had been so certain of winning that he had stopped to play and to nap along the way. Ben had attached a cotton ball to the seat of his blue jeans. "I am never ever embarrassed," he had said again, wiggling his behind with its fluffy white puff of a tail.

"I think we all know the moral of that fable," Mrs. Pidgeon said. *"Slow and steady wins the race!"*

Ben hip-hopped back to his desk, and Tricia slid her gloved feet slowly across the wooden floor until she reached hers.

"Me next? Oh, please, me next?" Barry Tuckerman, as usual, had his hand in the air.

"Do we have time for one more today?" Gooney Bird asked.

Mrs. Pidgeon nodded. "Just one," she said.

"Okay, Barry." Gooney Bird pointed to him.

"You can't be a bear!" Beanie said. "I already did bear!"

"Or a bunny," added Ben, who was turned around in his seat trying to remove his cotton-ball tail.

Barry Tuckerman came to the front of the room.

"He doesn't have a costume!" Malcolm called out. "You're supposed to have a costume! Barry doesn't have a—!"

Mrs. Pidgeon put her calm-down arm over Malcolm's shoulders. "Shhh," she said in a low voice. "Barry will explain."

Barry Tuckerman bowed to the class. "I have as much of a costume as Tricia did," he said. "She just had gloves.

"Tyrone only had a pie tin for dinosaur armor. And Ben just had a cotton-ball tail.

"You don't have to have *clothes* for a costume. I have this." He held up something silver and shiny.

The children all peered toward it, trying to see what the small shiny disk was. "It's money!" Keiko said.

"Correct," Barry replied. "It's five cents. It's a nickel."

"Why do you have a nickel?" asked Beanie.

"I'll explain in a minute. Anybody got a nickel?" Barry asked the class. Several children reached for their pockets. They shook their heads.

"I have two quarterth," Felicia Ann whispered. "The tooth fairy brought them."

"I have two pennies, in my shoes!" Chelsea announced. "See?" She held one foot up and the children could see that she was wearing loafers with pennies wedged into their slots for decoration.

Mrs. Pidgeon had taken her purse from the desk drawer. "I do, Barry!" she said. "I have a nickel!" She held it up.

"What's on it?" Barry asked. "Look carefully."

Mrs. Pidgeon examined her coin. "Let me see. On one side there's Thomas Jefferson. We all recognize him, don't we?" She pointed to the chart of United States presidents on the wall.

The second-graders nodded and looked at the portrait of the third president.

"He can't be Thomas Jefferson for his fable!" Malcolm shouted. "He can't be, can he? He can't! Because Thomas Jefferson's a guy and for a fable you have to be a—"

"Wait a minute, Malcolm," Mrs. Pidgeon said. "Let me turn my nickel over. Maybe there's a . . . No, it's a house. Here's Jefferson's beautiful big home on the other side. It was called Monticello."

"Big house!" Ben shouted. "B for big house? That's not an animal!"

Tyrone began to rap. *"Good ole Barry, he be actin' like a fool, cuz he don' pay attention when she tellin' the rule . . ."*

"Excuse me!" Barry said loudly, and Tyrone, with an apologetic smile, fell silent.

"Could I see that, please, Mrs. Pidgeon?" Barry asked. She handed him her coin.

"Well," he said, after he had examined it, "there are different kinds of nickels, I guess. And *mine* has a picture of a—"

He went to the board, picked up the chalk, and added his animal to the long list.

BUFFALO, Barry wrote neatly.

"Here is my fable," Barry announced. He opened his paper and read from it, holding his nickel up to the class with his other hand.

The American Buffalo

The correct scientific name for the American Buffalo is actually bison. The National Bison Association would like us to use the correct name for this magnificent beast.

Once there had been about 60 million bison in the American West from Canada to Mexico. But by 1893, there were only a little more than three hundred left.

Bison were the center of life for the Native Americans. They provided food, shelter, and clothing. But gradually—

"This isn't a story!" Malcolm called out. "Barry is supposed to be telling a story! It isn't a story about a buffalo!"

"It doesn't have a *suddenly*," Ben added. "It has a *gradually* instead!"

"It is too a story!" Barry replied angrily. "I learned all about it in the encyclopedia!"

Mrs. Pidgeon went to the front of the room, holding up her "Quiet, please" hand toward the class.

"Barry," she said, "you provided us with a real learning experience. I never knew there was a nickel with a buffalo—excuse me, *bison* — on it. And your report is very interesting. One of these days we will have a lesson about doing reports, and we will each have a chance to present one.

"But a report is *nonfiction*."

"What's that mean?" Barry asked. He was looking down at his nickel.

"Well, it means *facts*. And a story is made up, and uses your imagination." Mrs. Pidgeon looked out at the class. "Gooney Bird? Did you have your hand up?"

Gooney Bird nodded. "Barry can make his buffalo report into a story," she said. "It can be an absolutely true story, and it can have a *suddenly*."

"Barry?" Mrs. Pidgeon said. "Want to try that?"

"I could help you," Gooney Bird told him.

"Well, okay," Barry said. "But it should be about a bison, not a buffalo, because the National Bison Association prefers the correct name."

"*Bithon* thtarts with a B," Felicia Ann pointed out.

Barry nodded. He went to the board, erased the word BUF-FALO, and replaced it with BISON.

Gooney Bird Greene went to the front of the class and stood beside Barry. Today she was wearing bib overalls on top of a ruffled blouse, and a pearl necklace.

"It's a good idea to start out with the word *once*," she whispered to Barry.

Barry scrunched his nose. He took a deep breath.

Once over sixty million bison roamed the plains.

Gooney Bird nudged him. "That's nonfiction, still," she said. "Try this." She whispered a sentence to Barry.

Barry began again, using Gooney Bird's opening sentence.

Once a young bison lived with his herd on the plains of North America.

He paused and looked at the class. "Is that okay?" he asked. The second-graders nodded.

"How big was he?" asked Beanie.

"Did he have a name?" asked Chelsea.

"See?" Gooney Bird said to Barry. "They're getting interested in the character. That's an important thing, with a story."

Barry thought for a moment, and continued.

He didn't have a name. Some people liked to call him Buffalo, but the National Bison Association prefers—

"Wait a minute!" Barry interrupted himself. "I started making a report again, didn't I?"

Gooney Bird nodded. "Start over," she suggested. "We all make mistakes. But you're doing great."

Barry took another deep breath and began his fable again.

Once there was a young bison who lived with his herd. There were about eight hundred of them. They

roamed the plains, eating grass and enjoying the sun-
shine in summer. In winter, they liked the snow, too,
because they had thick fur and were never cold.

"Is that too reporty?" Barry asked Gooney Bird.

"No," she said. "Details are good. I liked knowing about the
thick fur because I could picture the bison in my imagination.

"But I'd add a little action to the story now," she said.

Barry nodded and went on.

One day when they were roaming and eating, roaming and eating, hunters with guns crept up on the
herd.

"Guns!" said Keiko, and covered her ears. "I don't want to
hear any more!"

"Blam!" shouted Malcolm, holding up his hand with his finger aimed like a gun. "Blam! Blam!" Mrs. Pidgeon went to
Malcolm's desk and put her calm-down arm across his shoulders.

"Maybe," Gooney Bird said to Barry, "some dialogue would
be good now."

Barry frowned. "Bison can't talk," he said.

"In stories they can," Gooney Bird explained. "That's the
good thing about stories. Anything can happen."

"Hmmm," Barry said. He was thinking.

Then he went on.

"Look!" called the young bison to his herd. "I see hunters coming!"

"Oh, dear!" an older bison said. "If they shoot us, the magnificent bison herds of the western plains may become extinct!"

"Yes," said another old bison, "once there were sixty million of us, but—"

Barry paused. He looked around. Keiko still had her hands over her ears. Malcolm was busy making a cootie-catcher out of paper. Beanie and Chelsea were beginning a game of tic-tac-toe. Mrs. Pidgeon, back at her desk, was grading their spelling tests.

"Time for a *suddenly*," Gooney Bird whispered to Barry.

"Yes," Barry agreed. He turned back to the class and spoke in a booming voice.

SUDDENLY

The second-graders looked up with interest. Barry grinned and continued.

Suddenly the hunters came riding out of the trees on their horses, shooting their guns, and shot a lot of the bison. Even the young one.

And after that there were practically no bison left in North America.

"That's the end," Barry said. "It's a sad ending."

"Some stories have sad endings," Gooney Bird announced. "It's good to be reminded of that."

Tricia raised her hand. "But what's the *moral?*" she asked.

Barry stood in front of the class with his arms folded across his chest. He thought and thought.

"Guns make a mess of things," he said finally.

9.

"One potato, two potato, three potato *four*," Gooney Bird chanted, moving back and forth between the clenched fists that Malcolm and Chelsea both held out.

"Out goes Y, O, U," she concluded, and Malcolm scowled, realizing he had lost.

"You'll get your turn next, Malcolm," Gooney Bird reassured him. "Anyway, it's supposed to be ladies before gentlemen.

"Chelsea? Your turn for a fable," Gooney Bird said, as Malcolm, still scowling, went back to his desk. "Malcolm, you'll be next."

Chelsea went up to the front of the class.

"I bet we all can guess what your animal will be," Mrs. Pidgeon said, chuckling, as Chelsea picked up the chalk. "It's so obvious."

Chelsea looked at Mrs. Pidgeon, and then at the class. "No, it isn't," she said. "No one will guess."

Mrs. Pidgeon grinned. "Cluck cluck cluck," she said.

"Cluck cluck cluck?" Chelsea repeated. "Excuse me?"

"Isn't your fable about a chicken?" Mrs. Pidgeon asked.

"Of course not. Who on earth would write a fable about a chicken? Chickens get their heads cut off, and then they get eaten," Chelsea said. She put her hands on her hips. "What kind of fable would *that* be?"

From her desk, Keiko groaned. "Oh, no!" she said. "Head cut off? *Eaten?*"

"Well, my goodness," Mrs. Pidgeon said. "I certainly blundered, didn't I? I thought I knew what you'd choose because of the 'ch' in your name. Chelsea equals chicken."

"Wrong," said Chelsea.

"But what other 'ch' animal is there?" Mrs. Pidgeon asked.

"Chipmunk!" called Beanie.

"Chimpanzee!" called Ben.

"Chinchilla!" called Barry.

"Chinchilla?" Gooney Bird asked. "What on earth is a chinchilla?"

"A small rodent from South America," Barry explained. "It looks like a rabbit, but with big mouselike ears and a squirrel-like tail. It was first introduced into the United States back in—"

He stopped. "I'm giving a report again," he said. "Sorry."

"Have you memorized the encyclopedia, Barry?" Mrs. Pidgeon asked, laughing.

"Almost," Barry said. "Only the A's, B's, and C's, though. I'm working on the D's now."

"And my fable is not about a single one of those animals," Chelsea announced. "Here is my costume." She took a small

63

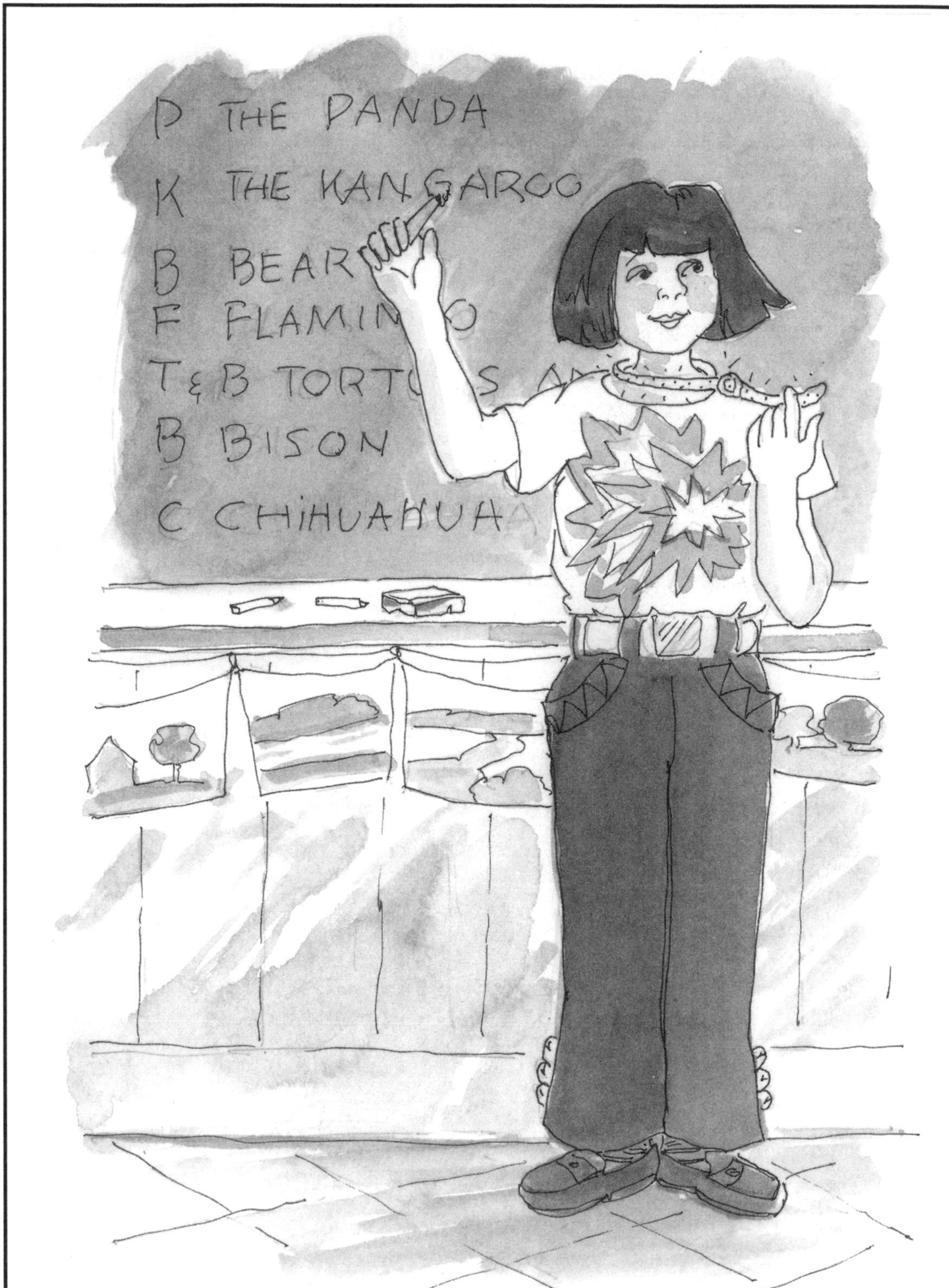
P THE PANDA
K THE KANGAROO
B BEAR
B BISON
C CHIHUAHUA

leather belt decorated with rhinestones out of her pocket. Carefully she buckled it around her neck.

Then she went to the board and, after checking her paper to be certain her spelling was correct, printed carefully: CHI-HUAHUA.

Tyrone made a face as he looked at the word. "Chi-hooah-hooah? I never heard of no chi-hooah-hooah!"

Chelsea explained. "It's a Spanish word. You say it this way: chi-wa-wa."

The second-graders all repeated it. *Chi-wa-wa.*

When she turned and held up her paper to read, Chelsea announced, "The title of my fable is just one word."

Woof

Once there was a teeny tiny dog called a Chihuahua. He lived in Mexico with a very rich lady.

He slept on a bed made out of one of her old mink coats. He had steak for dinner every single night. He had a collar with diamonds on it.

He was allowed to get on the furniture.

One day, when he was on the sofa, he looked through the window and saw many other dogs playing in the road. They were chasing one another, and biting sticks, and barking at cars.

"Woof!" he said, meaning that he wanted to go out and play with them.

"No, you must stay inside," said the rich lady. "Here. Have a cream puff and a glass of wine."

But the Chihuahua kept looking through the window. "Woof," he said again.

"Woof.

"Woof."

He kept saying it all day long, until the rich lady was so annoyed that she opened the door to the house and told him, "Okay then, go outside if you want to."

Off he went.

But when the bigger dogs saw him, they did not know what he was. Maybe a cat? Or maybe a chinchilla?

A chinchilla is a small rodent that lives in South America . . .

Chelsea paused. "Oh, dear," she said. "I started making a report."

"That's okay," Gooney Bird told her. "Please go on. Your fable is interesting. It has details, dialogue, and suspense."

So Chelsea continued.

The bigger dogs began to chase the Chihuahua. "Help! Help!" he cried, though in his language it sounded like "Woof! Woof!"

If the rich lady heard him, she paid no attention. She had listened to enough woofs that day. She was playing an opera on her stereo.

The Chihuahua ran as fast as he could on his teeny tiny legs. The bigger dogs kept chasing him. He was never seen again.

"That's the end," Chelsea said to the class.

"But what happened to him?" Beanie asked.

"No one knows," Chelsea explained.

"But a story has to have an ending!" Beanie complained.

"This story leaves you hanging," Gooney Bird told the class. "Some stories do."

"Oh, no!" Keiko wailed. *"Hanging?"*

"It just means—what's the word, Mrs. Pidgeon?" Gooney Bird asked.

"I think the word would be *ambiguous*," Mrs. Pidgeon said. "Let me look it up." She picked up her dictionary and leafed through the pages of the A's. "Here we are," she said. Then she read aloud, "'Open to many different interpretations.' Yes, Chelsea's story has an ambiguous ending."

The class was silent for a moment. They were all worrying about what might have happened to the Chihuahua.

They looked sad.

"Class," Gooney Bird suggested, "let's think about the moral of the Chihuahua story."

"What color wath the Chihuahua?" Felicia Ann asked shyly.

"Brown," Chelsea replied after she had thought for a minute, "with some spots near his tail."

"Well," Felicia Ann said, "the moral could be *Be proud of your color,* like my flamingo story."

"Yes, it could," Gooney Bird told her.

"I know! I know!" Beanie called, with her hand raised.

"Beanie?" Gooney Bird pointed to her.

"It could be *You don't have to be big or brave.* Like my bear fable."

"It could," said Gooney Bird.

"How about this?" Mrs. Pidgeon said. "Could it be *Sometimes what you already have is the best thing*? Like my panda fable?"

"It could," Gooney Bird said, and all of the second-graders nodded.

"Or my kangaroo story!" Keiko said. *"There's no place like home!"*

"Any one of the morals fits just fine," Gooney Bird pointed out. "Chelsea? What did you have in mind for the moral of your Chihuahua fable?"

Chelsea fingered the leather rhinestone-trimmed collar that was still buckled around her neck. "Here is the moral of my fable," she announced. *"Rich is good. If you have a mink coat, you should stay put."*

The classroom was silent.

Mrs. Pidgeon looked at her watch. "You know what?" she said. "It's lunchtime. And I'm hungry."

"Me, too!" Gooney Bird said. "And guess what! I have an anchovy sandwich today, on date-nut bread. I'll trade half if anyone wants."

10.

No one wanted half of Gooney Bird's sandwich. No one even wanted to sit near Gooney Bird's sandwich.

"Are you sure you wouldn't like some? Last chance," she said. "Keiko?"

"Not I," said Keiko.

"Nicholas?"

"Not I," said Nicholas.

"Barry?"

"Not I," said Barry.

"Tricia?"

"Not I," said Tricia.

The children began to giggle as they went around the table, answering one by one.

Gooney Bird tied her bib. "Well," she said, "in that case, I will eat it all myself." She took a bite and said, "Yum."

"We told the story of the Little Red Hen!" Chelsea said. "Cluck cluck cluck!"

"I can't believe Mrs. Pidgeon thought my fable was going to be about a chicken," she grumbled.

"Here, have a piece of fried chicken," Nicholas said, and handed her a crispy wing from his lunchbox. "Can I have your orange, for a trade?"

Chelsea considered that. "Okay," she said, and handed him her orange. She bit into the chicken wing. "Nobody would eat a Chihuahua," she said. "None of our fable animals are edible."

"Bear is," Beanie pointed out. "Some people eat bear."

"Yuck. Well, not panda, though, or kangaroo, or—what others did we have?"

"Bunny, and tortoise," Tricia said. "People eat those."

"And bison," Barry added. "Bison is a very healthful food. You should eat bisonburgers instead of hamburgers. Less cholesterol."

"Nobody would eat a flamingo," Felicia Ann said. "I think it would make you thick."

"How about T. rex?" asked Ben.

Tyrone, whose mouth was full of tuna fish sandwich, began to wiggle rhythmically in his seat. *"Teee rex, Teee rex,"* he murmured. *"See my muscles flex, if I munch on ol' T. rex . . . "* He lifted his arm and tried to demonstrate the muscle.

"How about Malcolm?" Tyrone asked suddenly, interrupting his own performance. "You didn't do your fable yet, Malcolm. Want me to make you up a rap? What animal you gonna do?"

Malcolm grinned. "Not telling," he said. "Secret. Surprise."

"Well," Gooney Bird pointed out, "your turn comes right

after lunch, Malcolm, so it won't be a surprise for long."

"How about Nicholas? Want a rap, Nicholas?" Tyrone was shifting back and forth in his chair, eager to dance.

"I'm going last," Nicholas said.

"You can't! Gooney Bird's going last! She already said so! *The day go fast, and Gooney Bird be last*—"

"Nicholas and I are doing our fable together," Gooney Bird explained. "Look what I have for dessert! A kumquat!" She held it up, and the other children examined it with interest.

"Kumquats are native to China," Barry announced, "although they are now cultivated in the United States. The kumquat tree is slow-growing and compact. Because of their thick rind, kumquats keep well and are easy to ship long distances."

"I thought you only read up through D in the encyclopedia, Barry," Gooney Bird said.

"I peeked into the K," he explained, "because I'm interested in kites."

"You're amazing." Gooney Bird bit into her kumquat.

"You can't do your fable with Gooney Bird, Nicholas," Ben said. "You're an N and she's a G."

"True," Gooney Bird replied. She grinned at Nicholas and Nicholas grinned back.

"Me and Gooney Bird have a surprise," Nicholas said.

Gooney Bird, imitating Mrs. Pidgeon, held up a grammar finger.

"Gooney Bird and I," Nicholas said. Then, to everyone's surprise, he chanted, *"You and I, me and you, we gotta surprise,*

oh yes we do . . ." He collected his crumpled paper napkin and an empty plastic cup. Then he shuffled over to the trash can, still chanting. Bruno, the Saint Bernard, lay dozing nearby.

"But first," Malcolm announced, rising from the table, "ME! My turn! I'm doing my fable next!"

With Malcolm eagerly leading the way, the second-graders walked back to the classroom. Bruno yawned, stood up slowly, and followed behind, hoping not to miss anything. His antlers were a little tilted.

11.

When the class was settled at their desks and Gooney Bird had announced that it was his turn to present his fable, Malcolm picked up a thick red marker and colored his own nose.

"A clown?" Keiko murmured.

Then Malcolm stood and attached something to his belt, twisting it around to the back. The children all watched, puzzled.

He walked to the front of the room.

Then, with his back turned to the class, he began to write on the board. The children were all still puzzled by the costume: his bright red nose and the sheet of purple construction paper dangling from his belt in the rear.

"Why is your nose red?" called Tricia.

"Why is your backside all purple?" asked Ben.

"Shhhh!" Mrs. Pidgeon said, holding up her quiet-please finger. "Let's see Malcolm's animal, and then maybe we'll understand his costume."

Carefully Malcolm wrote an uppercase M. Then an A. Then an N.

"NO FAIR!" Tyrone called. "He can't be a man!"

"You have to be an animal, Malcolm!" Barry said loudly. "Remember you thought I was Thomas Jefferson and it wasn't an animal? Isn't that right, Mrs. Pidgeon? Isn't that right, Gooney Bird?"

Malcolm had turned around and was looking impatiently at the second-graders.

"Well," Gooney Bird said, "a man is a mammal. Maybe a fable can be about any mammal."

"But mine wathn't a mammal," Felicia Ann pointed out. "Flamingo ith a bird."

"Neither was mine!" Tricia announced. "I was a tortoise. That's not a mammal."

"You're right." Gooney Bird looked as if she were thinking. "I don't know if there is a rule about fables. If we can have a bird, or a tortoise, or a T. rex, as the main character, maybe we could have a man."

"I wonder what Aesop would say," Mrs. Pidgeon said.

"And anyway, what's that purple thing on your backside, Malcolm?" Chelsea asked. "It's weird. So is your nose."

Malcolm grinned. He wrinkled his nose and wiggled his bottom. Then, when the class grew quiet, he turned and added some more letters on the board.

DRILL

He turned back to the class, wiggled his bottom again, then

lifted one arm and scratched with the other. "Oooh, oooh, oooh," Malcolm said, making an odd hooting sound.

"Mandrill!" Gooney Bird announced. "Malcolm is a mandrill!"

"But he's acting like a chimp, or a monkey," Beanie pointed out. Now Malcolm was leaping about, his legs bent, still making the sound.

"A mandrill is a kind of monkey, sort of," Gooney Bird explained. "Like a baboon, I think. I've seen them at the zoo. They're the ones with red noses and "

"Oh, no!" Keiko squealed. "The ones with the yucky bright blue and pink bottoms! I *hate* those!" She made a face.

Malcolm stopped jumping around. He announced his fable's title.

The Mandrill and Its Young

Once there was a female mandrill who was expecting a baby. She got very fat. Then one day her baby was born. It was pretty cute. She liked it.

But then, suddenly, she had *another* baby.

And then, suddenly, *another.*

Well. That was pretty surprising. Now she had three mandrill babies. They were very noisy. They wanted to be fed every minute. They made a big mess. They threw things and broke things.

The father mandrill was never home. Sometimes the mother was so nervous and tired that she screamed.

And the worst thing was, the mother mandrill didn't have any time to take care of her older mandrill child.

"Oh, I wish I could get rid of a couple of these babies," she said. "Maybe I can sell them."

She asked all around the jungle, but no one wanted to buy a baby mandrill.

"Well, maybe I can give them away," she thought.

But no one wanted those babies, even as a gift.

She couldn't figure out what to do. She sat on the jungle floor, thinking.

Suddenly one of the babies smiled at her.

Then the next one did.

And then the third. All three baby mandrills were smiling for the first time.

"Hey, look!" the mother said to her older mandrill child. He was up in a tree, hiding, because he hated the babies. But he came down when his mom called.

He looked at the smiles. He reached over and tickled one of the babies. It laughed.

Another one puckered up its mouth and blew him a kiss.

The third one climbed into his lap, curled up, and began to sleep very quietly.

The older mandrill child was surprised at how much, suddenly, he had begun to like the babies.

"Let's keep them," he said to his mother. "They're cute."

So they did. After that, when the babies cried, the

mother mandrill and her older mandrill child just covered their ears. They knew it wouldn't last.

"Oh, I love that fable," Keiko said with a sigh. "It was so sweet."

"Yeth," said Felicia Ann. "Tho thweet."

"Did the babies have purple bums?" asked Tyrone.

Malcolm shrugged. "I guess so," he said. "They were mandrills."

Gooney Bird went to the front of the class. "There is nothing whatsoever wrong with a purple bottom," she said. "Colorful is always good. I'm planning on dyeing part of my hair purple sometime.

"Thank you for your fable, Malcolm. Do you want to tell us the moral?"

"Okay. It's this," Malcolm said. *Things get better.*

"They do indeed," Mrs. Pidgeon said, smiling. "And it sounds as if things are getting better at your house, Malcolm."

He nodded happily. Then he stopped smiling. "It'll be bad when I get home today, though," he said. "My mom will scream."

"Why is that?" asked Mrs. Pidgeon.

"Because I used an indelible marker on my nose," Malcolm said.

12.

"Who's left?" Mrs. Pidgeon looked around the room. "Just Gooney Bird and Nicholas, I guess. Goodness, we've done a lot of fables!"

"When do we do the parade?" Beanie asked.

"Tomorrow. It's the last day of school before vacation. Have you all saved your costumes? I have my panda vest right here in my desk drawer."

The children all nodded.

"Can I do us a rap for the parade?" Tyrone asked. "Most parades got a band. We need some kind of music."

"Yes!" the children called. "A rap!"

"Of course," said Mrs. Pidgeon. "But we'll all need to learn it, Tyrone, and we don't have much time."

"Ain't no problem, nuthin' to learn, just follow me and take your turn . . ." Tyrone chanted.

"All right, I guess we can do that," said Mrs. Pidgeon. "We'll have a little practice time before we start the parade." She looked toward the corner of the classroom. "Gooney Bird?

Nicholas? Are you ready?"

Gooney Bird and Nicholas had been whispering to each other in the corner by the gerbil cage, planning the presentation of their fable. Now they nodded and came to the front of the room. Nicholas was grinning. It was already hard to remember how sad he had been, how he had stopped eating, and how he had sulked and refused to discuss his fable just a few days before.

They stood side by side and put on their costumes, dark beards that attached by plastic pieces that hooked around their ears.

"They're being Abe Lincoln!" Ben called. "That's not fair!"

"Anyway," Barry pointed out, "Abe Lincoln is A and L! They're supposed to be G and N!"

Gooney Bird held up a quiet-please finger. Eventually the class calmed down, though some of the children were still laughing at the sight of Gooney Bird and Nicholas wearing the dark brown beards, which did not match Gooney Bird's bright red hair, or Nicholas's blond curls, at all.

"We are not Abe Lincoln," Gooney Bird told the class. Her beard wobbled a little as she talked. "We are two animals who live in a large herd on the plains of Africa. Nicholas, will you write our name on the board?"

The list on the board was very long by now. Nicholas had to lean down to add the final animal at the end of it. Carefully, with the chalk, he made a capital G.

"I *knew* you were going to let Nicholas cheat!" Malcolm called. "He can't be a G animal!"

"Wait, Nicholas," Gooney Bird said. "Do not write any more until I deal with this." She put her hands on her hips and looked sternly at Malcolm.

"Malcolm," she said, "it is very important to have all the information before you come to a conclusion.

"For example," she went on, "if a stranger looked at you, that stranger might think, 'That poor boy has a very bad cold. See how bright pink his nose is.' "

"I don't have a cold," Malcolm argued.

"Of course you don't. The stranger wouldn't have all the information. The stranger wouldn't know that your very pink nose was a leftover mandrill."

"My mom scrubbed it," Malcolm said.

"Nonetheless," Gooney Bird replied, "do you see what I mean, about needing the information?"

"I guess so," Malcolm said. He rubbed his nose.

"Nicholas," Gooney Bird said, "please continue."

Nicholas, holding his beard out of the way with one hand, printed the remaining letters: N U.

"The title of our fable is 'Two Gnus,'" Gooney Bird announced.

"The G is silent," she added.

"If we were doing a story about medieval times," Nicholas said, "I could be a knight, because the K is silent!"

Malcolm frowned. "When does an M get to be silent?" he asked.

"I don't believe an M is ever silent," Gooney Bird said.

"*Malcolm* is never silent," Barry added.

"G's are special," Nicholas said proudly, "and they make my N special."

"Tho thecial," Felicia Ann said with a happy smile.

"Class," Mrs. Pidgeon announced, "maybe after vacation, maybe in January, we will do a whole unit about silent letters, and let's see, homonyms, and synonyms, and—oh yes— *palindromes;* those are especially interesting. But right now, it is time for a fable."

Gooney Bird and Nicholas, side by side, wearing their beards, unfolded their papers and read their fable together.

Two Gnus

Once there were two gnus, a female gnu and a male gnu. They were friends. Both had beards. All gnus, female and male, have beards.

They were part of a large herd and they moved slowly across the African plains, eating grasses.

Several lions were watching them and making plans for an attack.

"Oh, no!" said Keiko.

"It's okay," Gooney Bird reassured her. "It has a happy ending. Just a little suspense, and a *suddenly*."

The fable continued. Keiko looked nervous but she was quiet.

The lions decided to attack late at night, when it was dark and the gnus were asleep. They planned to carry

away several young gnus and have them all for breakfast the next morning.

Gooney Bird looked over at Keiko and whispered, "It's okay.
Don't worry."

The lions decided to rest for the early part of the
night, so that they would have lots of energy for the
big attack. They curled up in a heap in the tall grass
and slept. They didn't need an alarm clock. Lions are
very good at knowing when to wake up.

The gnus gathered in their herd and prepared to
sleep, too. But they were thirsty. It was a time of
drought.

"*Drought* has a silent G *and* a silent H," Gooney Bird
pointed out to the class. "But we'll talk about those next
month."

"Are you *sure* there's no silent M?" Malcolm asked.

"Almost positive," Gooney Bird said. Malcolm scowled.

Suddenly the chief gnu sniffed the air and smelled
some water far ahead.

"We really need water," he murmured softly. "We
haven't had water in a long time. I think maybe we
should skip tonight's sleep and move forward to get a
drink."

He made the special gestures, tossing his head and

stamping his foot, that told the entire herd to get moving. And off they went, some of them yawning because they had been almost asleep.

In the middle of the night, at the very darkest time, the lions, who were very rested now and full of energy, woke up. "Time to attack!" the chief lion (a female, by the way. It is always the females who do the hunting. The males are very lazy) announced. "Gnu for breakfast!

"Go!" she said. And the lions leapt out of the tall grass, in attack mode, and dashed to the place where the gnus had been.

But the vast plain was empty. Oh, there was a snake slithering past, and a couple of vultures sitting on the branch of one crummy-looking tree. But the herd of gnus had disappeared. They were far away, having a nice drink of water.

"Bummer," said the lions. "We'll have to have that old leftover zebra for breakfast."

"The end," said Gooney Bird and Nicholas together. They bowed, and the class clapped.

"Good fable!" Mrs. Pidgeon said, getting up from her chair. "And I suppose the moral is something about being watchful and vigilant?"

Gooney Bird and Nicholas shook their heads. "Here's the moral," they said together. *No gnus is good news.*

13.

"May I march with you?" Mr. Leroy asked.

The children of Mrs. Pidgeon's second grade were lining up in the school hallway on Friday afternoon, the last day of school before the holiday vacation. They all had their bits and pieces of costumes on, and wore nametags revealing the names of their animals. They were wiggling and giggling and shuffling their feet and practicing chanting the rap that Tyrone had prepared for the parade.

"Ask Gooney Bird," Beanie told the principal. "She's in charge."

Gooney Bird Greene was at the head of the parade, wearing her beard and a pair of plaid pajamas. "Well," she said dubiously when Mr. Leroy asked permission to join the group, "we're all animals. You have to be an animal. And," she added, looking at his suit, "you have to have some kind of costume. See Mrs. Pidgeon, in her black shirt and white vest? She's a panda.

"And I'm a gnu," she added, stroking her beard, in case he hadn't already read her nametag or figured it out. "The animal has to begin with the first letter of your name. Gnu has a silent G."

"Yes, I understand," the principal said. "I was in your classroom when Tyrone did the T. rex fable. But I think I can fulfill the requirement. My first name is John: a J. But my middle name is Thomas, so I do have a T, as well. And look! Here's my costume!"

He flipped his necktie, today a bright green one with candy canes on it, so that it dangled in front of his buttoned suit jacket.

"Can I be a tiger? Get it? Tie-ger?" he asked.

Gooney Bird sighed. She put her hands on her hips. "If you were in second grade, Mr. John Thomas Leroy," she told him, "I would tell you that you are trying to bend the rules just a *little* too far. But since you're the principal, I'm going to say yes. You may march."

"Thank you, Gooney Bird." Mr. Leroy turned to find a place in the line.

"Alphabetical!" Gooney Bird called to him. "We're lining up alphabetically. "You'll go back there"—she thought for a moment, then pointed—"after panda and before tortoise.

"I should be there with Nicholas, behind the flamingo," she explained, "but since I'm the leader, I'm marching in front."

"Why isn't Nicholas between kangaroo and mandrill?" Mr. Leroy asked, after he had looked around.

"Oh, Mr. Leroy, it's a very long story," Gooney Bird told him.

"Ready? Let's go!" Gooney Bird called.

"Startin' with a gnu, and we goin' right thru . . ." the children chanted, along with Mrs. Pidgeon, and, after a moment, Mr. Leroy, who had to listen first to grasp the words, since he had not been there for the rehearsal.

The parade, with Gooney Bird leading, began to shuffle and dance down the hall toward the multipurpose room. The other schoolchildren were there waiting, but Mr. Furillo stood in the hall with his large push broom. *"Goin' right through!"* the custodian joined in, giving his broom a few rhythmic swishes on the tile floor.

Bruno, the Saint Bernard, who had been asleep near the utility closet door, was startled awake. He looked terrified. Quickly he rose to his feet, dropped his tail between his legs, and loped off toward the administration office, where he could hide.

Cute little bear, he got brown hair. . .
Here come the bison, as big as Mike Tyson. . .
Laugh at the bunny if you think he be funny. . .

One by one, alphabetically, they chanted the animal names and the rhyming rap that came so easily to Tyrone. As the parade entered the multipurpose room, the audience of waiting children cheered and clapped. Gooney Bird twirled in a dance step and then gestured to the classes to join in the chant. "Repeat after us!" she called.

Chihuahua, he be teeny, like a piece a scaloppine. . .

89

Chelsea, wearing her rhinestone collar, danced forward as the room full of children repeated the chant about the Chihuahua.

Next Felicia Ann, dressed again in bright pink, twirled while the second-graders chanted, *"Flamingo's legs be brown, she don' wanna put 'em down . . ."* and the rest of the school repeated it. Then,

> *Got us a gnu, and got us another,*
> *'Cuz the first gnu's a girl and she got her a brother . . .*

Gooney Bird and Nicholas did a special little gnu dance while the children clapped.

Betcha thought nuthin' would make a rhyme with gnu,
But here she be, and her name be kangaroo . . .

Keiko giggled and did a hopping little kangaroo dance. The parade continued shuffling around the room while the entire school clapped in rhythm.

Panda be a babe who be eatin' bamboo,
She be black and white all over and she don't got no tat-
too . . .

Mrs. Pidgeon held out her arms and did a bit of a waltz, but the children were all looking toward the doorway, where Mr. Furillo was standing with his broom. He grinned and held up his right arm so they could see his tattoo of a dagger and snake.

Here come tiger, he be one fierce dude,
He scare everybody wif his attitude . . .

Principal Leroy, who just that morning had made a speech about school budgets to the Watertower Rotary Club at their monthly breakfast meeting, now did a lunging dance across the center of the floor, and growled loudly before he moved back into the parade line and resumed shuffling.

Mr. Tortoise be so dumb an' slow,
He dunno when to start and he dunno when to go . . .

Tricia, laughing, waved her big leather gloves and did a very slow dance while the children repeated the tortoise chant.

Then, finally, Tyrone moved out of the parade line and all of the children cheered. He turned a somersault, spun in a circle on his back, and then jumped to his feet and started the T. rex part of the rap:

Mr. T. rex big but he dunno how to think,
'Cuz his brain be small, and he go extinct . . .

"He go extinct," repeated all the children and teachers. Tyrone continued:

> *This be the end of our fabulous parade*
> *But there plenty more stories out there to be made*
> *'Cuz ol' Mr. Aesop, he be a winner—*
> *Now we all go home and eat our dinner!*

"Turkey!" said Tyrone later, as the children were putting on their coats. "That's a T. I could do a rap about holiday food!"

"Cranberry sauce! That's a C!" said Chelsea. "Or celery!" She pulled her mittens out of her pockets.

"M for mashed potatoes!" Malcolm announced, zipping his jacket.

"I could be beans!" said Ben as he pulled on his boots.

"Or beets!" suggested Beanie.

"Uh-oh." Tyrone pointed. "Look at Nicholas."

Nicholas, who had been winding his scarf around his neck, was suddenly very still. He looked distressed.

Gooney Bird had removed her beard. She was wearing the sheared-beaver jacket that she sometimes borrowed from her mother. Carefully she wrapped a long scarf around her neck with a flourish. Then she went over to him. "Nicholas," she said sympathetically, "do not even worry about this for one second. We are *not* doing a food rap. We are all going home to enjoy the holidays.

"Right?" She looked around.

"Right," the other children agreed.

"Okay, right," said Tyrone, reluctantly.

"Even though," Gooney Bird said with a grin, "I would be gravy."